A CHILD'S EYE VIEW OF
HISTORY

Discover history through the experiences of children from the past

WRITTEN BY **Fiona Macdonald**

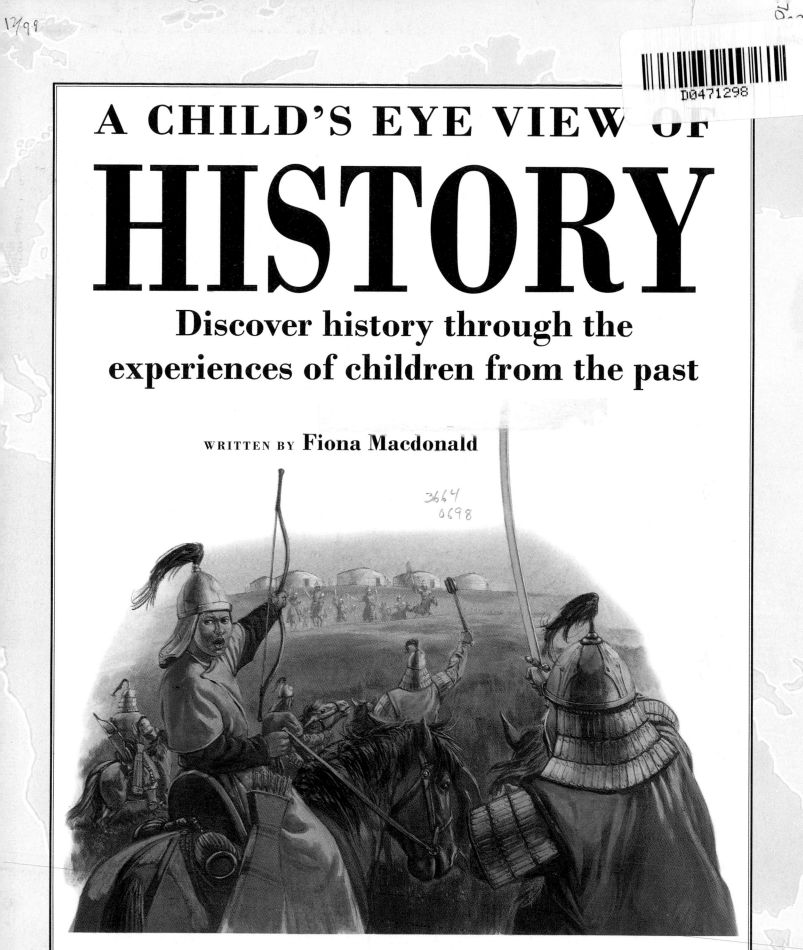

SIMON & SCHUSTER BOOKS FOR YOUNG READERS

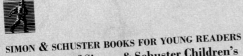

SIMON & SCHUSTER BOOKS FOR YOUNG READERS
An imprint of Simon & Schuster Children's
Publishing Division
1230 Avenue of the Americas, New York,
New York 10020

Copyright © 1998 by Marshall Editions
Developments Ltd.
All rights reserved including the right of
reproduction in whole or in part in any
form.

SIMON & SCHUSTER BOOKS FOR YOUNG READERS
is a trademark of Simon & Schuster.

This book was conceived, edited, and
designed by
Marshall Editions
170 Piccadilly, London W1V 9DD

First American Edition, 1998
Originated by Chroma Graphics
Printed and bound in Italy
10 9 8 7 6 5 4 3 2 1

Library of Congress Cataloging-in-Publication Data
Macdonald, Fiona
     A child's eye view of history / written by Fiona
Macdonald.—1st American ed.
        p.   cm.
     Includes index.
     ISBN 0-689-81378-3
     1. World history—Juvenile literature.   1. Title.
D20.M25   1998
909-dc21
97-10507
CIP
AC

Editor: Katrina Maitland Smith
Designer: Ed Simkins
Managing Editor: Kate Phelps
Design Manager: Ralph Pitchford
Art Director: Branka Surla
Editorial Director: Cynthia O'Brien
Production: Janice Storr, Selby Sinton
Researcher: Lynda Wargen
Picture Researcher: Elaine Willis

The publishers would like to thank
Khayakazi Khatwya and Thembile Pepeteka
for their invaluable contribution to page 56,
and Inder Malhotra and the British Library
for their kind permission to use material
from a recorded interview for Trevor Royle's
book Last Days of the Raj on page 54.

CONTENTS

CONTENTS

INTRODUCTION

Few children are featured in history books. This is rather surprising when you think that, in almost all periods of history, over half the people living in the world were under twenty-one years old. And all men and women—rich or poor, famous or unknown—were once children themselves. Why do we know so little about their early years?

▲ *A statue of ancient Egyptian pharaoh Tuthmosis III shows him with the beard and headdress that were the signs of royal power.*

Most children were not thought to be important. In many past civilizations, only a few people had power. Kings, queens, and nobles ruled vast empires, commanded armies, and often owned most of the land. Their actions affected thousands or even millions of people's lives, and they were very famous. We know a lot about them because they employed scribes, officials, and artists to record their achievements and to create portraits of them.

We know a little about royal children because the same scribes and artists wrote about them and made their portraits, too. Royal children were considered important because they would have power one day. Scribes wrote about a few other famous children, such as athletes, but the lives of ordinary people and their children were usually ignored. They had little money and hardly any power, so few writers or artists thought it worthwhile to record their lives. So we know much less about them.

◀ *Painted pottery like this Greek vase made in about 500 B.C. gives us a lot of information about ancient life.*

▶ *This picture of a Creek lacrosse game is based on eyewitness descriptions by travelers visiting Native American lands, and on the memories of Creek elders.*

We don't even have much that was written by children themselves about their lives because, in the past, most children could not write. There was hardly any free schooling, and only children from noble or wealthy families learned how to read or write.

It was not until about 1600 in Europe and America that children began writing letters to friends and families. They also began to keep their own diaries. So it is only over the last few hundred years that we start to know what some children felt and thought about their lives from their own writings.

◀ *Two pages from a Mayan codex (folding book) from more than one thousand years ago contain pictures of gods and kings as well as lists of important events.*

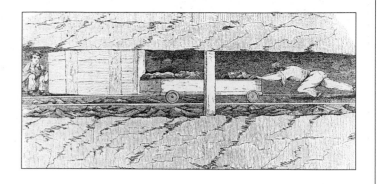

▲ *A picture from a government report in the 1830s shows the appalling conditions children suffered at work in England.*

These are some of the reasons why we know little about children's lives in the past. Over the last fifty years, however, historians have become interested in all people in the past, not just the rich and powerful. They have been gathering information from many different sources to find out about adults and children from across the world and from all areas of life. Sources such as inscriptions, official records, poems, paintings, sculpture, letters, and diaries all provide clues to the lives of people, and have helped piece together the experiences of the children in the pages of this book.

Today, in many countries, a lot of things, such as books, clothes, and films are made for children. There are children's play areas, children's libraries, and children's hospitals. But, for a long time, there was no separate "world of childhood" for artists and writers to record. From the age of about five, children wore adult-style clothes and, as soon as they were able, they helped with their family's work.

▼ *This sixteenth-century painting shows the stiff and elaborate clothes that children from wealthy families had to wear at that time.*

◀ *We know what German artist Albrecht Dürer looked like when he was young because he drew this portrait of himself in 1484 when he was thirteen years old.*

• Where the book includes words written or spoken by the children themselves—or by other people about the children—the language has been adjusted for the modern reader.

ANCIENT EGYPT

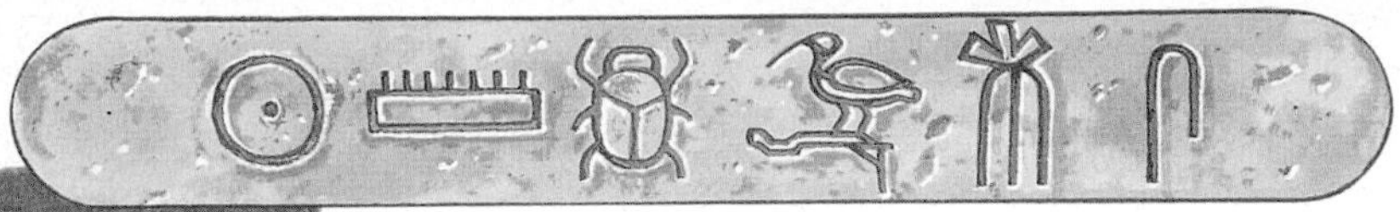

▲ *This is Tuthmosis III's name carved in hieroglyphics—the ancient Egyptian picture writing used in ceremonial inscriptions.*

TUTHMOSIS III was ten years old when he became king of Egypt in 1489 B.C. But for the first twenty years of his reign, Tuthmosis was not allowed to rule. His stepmother, Hatshepsut, governed the country in his place. As a child, he had to go with her on royal tours through the kingdom or to visit the magnificent temple she was building at Deir el-Bahri in the pharaohs' royal burial ground, the Valley of the Kings.

Tuthmosis at last began to rule in 1469 B.C., after Hatshepsut died. He then became one of Egypt's greatest pharaohs. He was a good lawmaker, a clever politician, and a brilliant battle-commander. By the end of his reign, in 1436 B.C., Egypt had become the most powerful nation in the Mediterranean and north African lands.

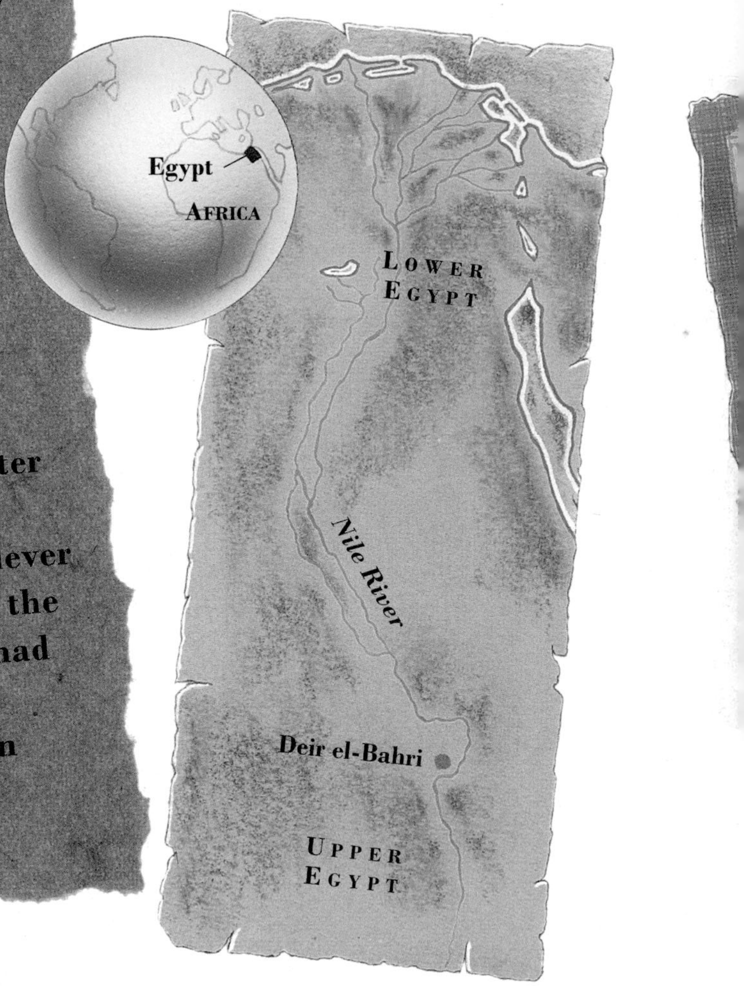

A statue of Tuthmosis III

Egypt
AFRICA

LOWER EGYPT

Nile River

Deir el-Bahri

UPPER EGYPT

▲ *The kingdom of Egypt was vast, but most of it was empty desert. Everyone lived on narrow strips of land on either side of the Nile River.*

▼ *Young Tuthmosis III went to the royal palace school. He learned how to read hieroglyphs (see left), and to write on papyrus (paper made from reeds) using a reed stalk as a pen, and ink made from soot mixed with glue.*

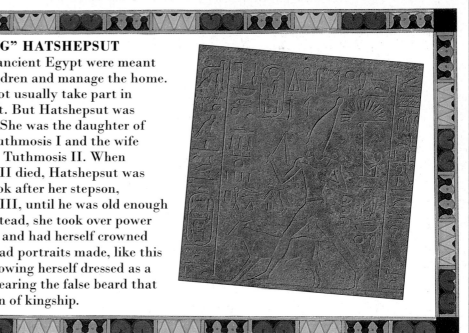

"KING" HATSHEPSUT

Women in ancient Egypt were meant to bear children and manage the home. They did not usually take part in government. But Hatshepsut was ambitious. She was the daughter of Pharaoh Tuthmosis I and the wife of Pharaoh Tuthmosis II. When Tuthmosis II died, Hatshepsut was asked to look after her stepson, Tuthmosis III, until he was old enough to rule. Instead, she took over power completely and had herself crowned king. She had portraits made, like this carving, showing herself dressed as a man and wearing the false beard that was the sign of kingship.

THE KINGDOM OF EGYPT

The lands of Upper and Lower Egypt were brought under the same rule by King Menes in about 3100 B.C., to form the huge kingdom of Egypt. Ancient Egyptian civilization flourished for the next 3,000 years until Egypt was conquered by the Romans in 30 B.C. The pharaoh, or king, was head of the Egyptian government and chief priest. He was honored as if he were a god. The Egyptian empire was strictly organized—well-trained scribes and officials worked for the government, administering laws and collecting taxes. They also organized peasants to work on massive building projects, producing richly decorated pyramids, temples, and tombs.

▼ *Hatshepsut's chief adviser and architect was Senenmut. He ran the royal palaces and taught Hatshepsut's daughter, Neferure, who sits in his arms in this statue.*

◀ *Like most pharaohs, Hatshepsut began to build a huge temple in memory of her reign as soon as she came to power. It was surrounded by gardens.*

ANCIENT GREECE

ALCIMIDAS OF AEGINA came from a famous sporting family. Many of his ancestors had been victorious at the games at Olympia, Corinth, Delphi, and Nemea. Like other young athletes, Alcimidas trained hard for a whole year before the games and ate a special diet, which included lots of meat. He competed in the Olympic Games, probably in 464 B.C., but he did not win anything. However, in 463 B.C., after several tough contests, Alcimidas won the boys' under-eighteen wrestling championship at the Nemean Games. He was honored as a hero by the citizens back home. The Greek poet Pindar wrote a poem to praise him. "Look," wrote Pindar, "Here comes the athlete boy. . . . Let us salute this winner with a glorious verse of song. It will last, and proclaim his noble deeds long after he and all his family have passed away."

◀▲ The rules of Greek wrestling allowed many dangerous holds and throws (above). This Greek storage jar (left) is decorated with a picture of pankration wrestling. In the pankration, everything except biting and gouging out eyes was allowed. The referee stands on the far left.

▼ More than 200 different sports meetings were held in lands around the Mediterranean Sea, but the most important took place in southern Greece.

EUROPE
Greece

GREECE
Delphi
Nemea   Corinth   Athens
Olympia   Aegina
Sparta
Sites of major games
N

GREECE AND THE GAMES

Ancient Greek civilization was at its most powerful between about 750 B.C. and 350 B.C. in mainland Greece, along the west coast of Turkey, and on the hundreds of islands nearby. Greek people were farmers, fishermen, and skilled craftspeople, who lived in communities known as city-states (a city and the fields and farms nearby). The city-states were rivals and were often at war. Athens was the richest and most powerful city-state.

The first Olympic Games was probably held in 776 B.C. Like all Greek festivals, its purpose was to honor the gods. It took place every four years and became the most important sports festival in all of Greece. Foreigners were not allowed to attend, but athletes from all over Greece, and from Greek colonies in many Mediterranean lands, traveled long distances to take part.

▼ *Only boys from wealthy families went to school in ancient Greece. They learned to read and write, recite poetry, sing, and play musical instruments such as the lyre (a small harp) and the flute. They were also taught sports; children were encouraged to have "a healthy mind in a healthy body."*

▲ *This statue shows a Greek girl playing with her pet cat. Children in ancient Greece were expected to work hard. Boys were trained by their parents in craft skills and farmwork. Girls learned childcare and housekeeping.*

▼ *Victorious athletes like Alcimidas were rewarded with prizes of valuable olive oil and fine cloth for new clothes. They were crowned with garlands of leaves and took part in a special victory parade.*

WOMEN AND SPORTS

At Olympia there were special games for women only, which were held in years when there were no games for men. Otherwise Greek women were not usually allowed to take part in public sports—or even attend as spectators. If they did, the punishment could be death. However, in one city-state, called Sparta, women and girls—like the girl runner shown in this small bronze statue—were forced to take part in sports. The city government believed it would make them give birth to stronger, healthier sons.

ANCIENT ROME

The Roman writer, Pliny the Younger

On August 24, A.D. 79, the volcano Vesuvius erupted, spewing out clouds of steam, poisonous gas, and ash. The town of Pompeii was covered with a layer of ash and mud thirteen feet deep.

Pliny the Younger was seventeen years old when it happened. He was staying with his mother and uncle on the other side of the Bay of Naples. Early in the afternoon his mother saw a huge, dirty cloud across the bay. Then a sailor arrived, saying that villagers were trapped by lava pouring out of the volcano. Pliny's uncle was commander of the Roman fleet. He set sail across the bay to save the villagers. But, like many others, he was choked to death by poisonous gases. The next day an earthquake forced Pliny and his mother to leave the coast. They hurried inland, followed by a terrified crowd. Many people believed that these events were the end of the world.

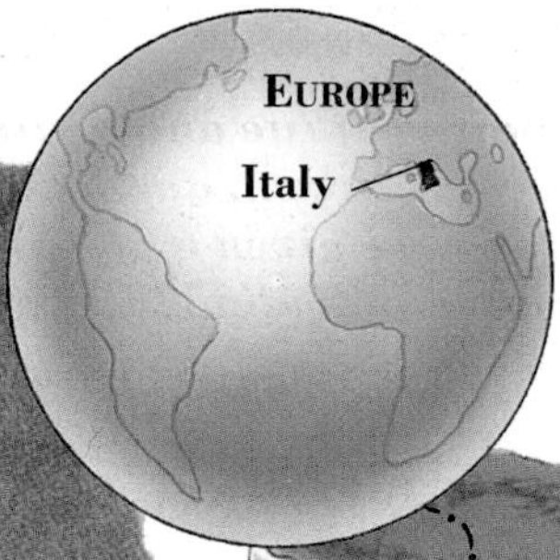

▼ The city of Rome was founded in 753 B.C. By A.D. 100, it was the center of an empire stretching from Scotland to the Black Sea. Everyone in the empire had to pay taxes to Rome and obey Roman laws.

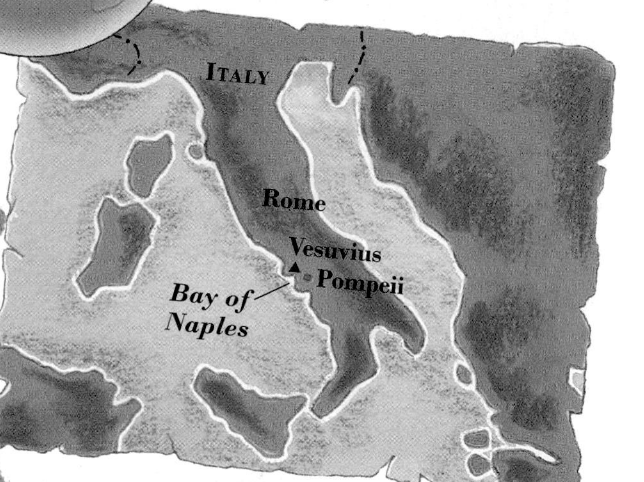

EUROPE
Italy

ITALY
Rome
Vesuvius
Pompeii
Bay of Naples

▼ When Vesuvius erupted, the sky went black for two days. From across the bay people watched as the sky lit up from time to time with flashes of fire and sheets of lightning. The sea heaved and churned, and the ground shook underfoot.

◀ *According to Roman law, fathers were the head of the family. They had the power of life and death over their wives, children, and slaves. Baby boys were given a good luck charm called a "bulla" to wear around their necks.*

THE ROMAN EMPIRE

The Romans lived in Italy. At first they were farmers, ruled by kings. In 509 B.C., the city of Rome became a republic, governed by officials who were elected (chosen) by the citizens. The citizens helped plan government policy and make new laws. Rome grew rich and strong— it had fine buildings, fresh water, cheap entertainment, and food for the poor. The well-trained Roman army began to conquer more land, and by about 220 B.C., the Romans ruled all of Italy. Over the next 300 years, they gained control of a vast empire overseas.

In 31 B.C., quarrels among leading citizens led to a civil war, and from 27 B.C., Rome was ruled by emperors. Some were wise and fair; others were weak and cruel. Roman power collapsed in A.D. 476, after the city was attacked by fierce warrior tribes from central Asia.

ROMAN EDUCATION

Roman boys from wealthy families started lessons when they were six or seven years old. They learned simple math, reading, and writing using a stylus (a pointed stick) and a wax tablet (*left*). From eleven or twelve years old, boys went to secondary school, where they studied Greek and Roman literature, history, arithmetic, and astronomy. After the age of sixteen, a few teenagers, like Pliny the Younger (*below*), continued their education by taking lessons from private tutors. Girls, and children from poor families, did not go to school.

▼ *Like many people in Pompeii, this dog was suffocated by poisonous gases from Vesuvius. The dog was chained up when the volcano erupted, and it died struggling to free itself. Its body was covered with layers of volcanic ash.*

TOYS AND GAMES

CHILDREN IN THE PAST PLAYED WITH TOYS that are surprisingly similar to those we have today. For thousands of years, babies have had pull-along toys on wheels, and girls and boys have played with balls and yo-yos. Just like today's dolls, ancient Egyptian and Native American dolls wore the clothes and hairstyles that were the latest fashion among the peoples who made them. And many clockwork toys made over fifty years ago were designed to look like the newest and most exciting cars and army equipment of the time.

Toys were fun but they could also help children learn skills that would be useful in their adult lives. Playing with toy boomerangs helped Aboriginal children learn how to hunt. African board games were useful for training the mind—helping fighters and hunters to plan ahead and be cunning.

Parents have always made toys for their children using materials they have around them. In the past, animal skins were made into dolls, clay was shaped into model animals, and nuts, pebbles, and seeds were used as counters for board games.

▼ This doll belonged to a girl from the Sioux Native American people who lived during the 1800s. The doll wears a deerskin dress decorated with fringes, glass beads that came from traders, and beads cut from porcupine quills.

◄ About five hundred years ago, an Aztec craftsperson in Mexico made this pottery pull-along dog on wheels.

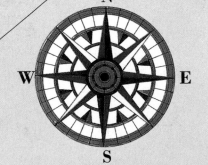

▼ *This toy car and driver, made of brightly painted metal, was made in Germany in the early 1900s. It was powered by clockwork wound up with a key.*

▲ *Japanese and Chinese people have been making some of the best kites in the world for thousands of years. These people in nineteenth-century Japan were flying kites to celebrate New Year's Day.*

▶ *Children have played with yo-yos for thousands of years. This boy and his yo-yo was pictured on a Greek vase made around 450 B.C.*

▼ *Aboriginal boys in Australia played with small boomerangs like this. It took lots of practice to throw the boomerang correctly so that it flew in a circle and returned to the thrower's hand.*

◀ *This wooden toy, shaped like a lion, was made in Egypt over 3,500 years ago. When you pull the string, its jaw snaps shut!*

◀ *Adults and children in Africa still play this board game, called mancala. Nuts, seeds, or painted pebbles are used for counters and players try to win all the counters, leaving their opponents with none.*

THE MAYA

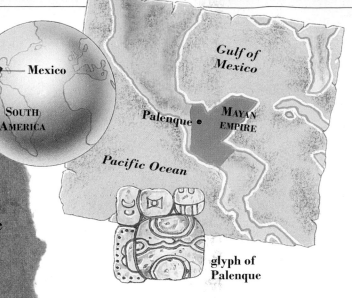

glyph of Palenque

A stone head of Lord Pacal on the day he became king

LORD PACAL became king of the Mayan city-state of Palenque in A.D. 615, when he was only twelve years old. Pacal's name means "shield." As king, it was his duty to be strong and warlike and to protect his people from attack. Pacal reigned for an astonishing sixty-eight years and made the city of Palenque rich and powerful. He built a magnificent temple, in which he was buried. Its walls were decorated with carvings of his ancestors—like all Mayan rulers, Pacal believed he was descended from the gods.

Each Mayan ruler was chosen at an important religious ceremony, often when he or she was still a young child. Prisoners of war were led in front of the chosen king or queen and were sacrificed one by one. As the blood of the captives was sprinkled around, the Mayans asked the gods to bless their future ruler.

▲ The Maya lived in the lush tropical rain forests in the far south of present-day Mexico. Their civilization flourished from about A.D. 250 to A.D. 900.

▲ Lord Pacal lived in the splendid royal palace at Palenque. The high tower was added by a later Mayan king for studying the stars.

MAYAN KINGDOMS

The Mayan lands were divided into several small kingdoms, each ruled by a king who was honored like a god. To display their wealth and power, Mayan kings built splendid capital cities full of fine stone buildings decorated with paintings and carvings.

Each capital city controlled the surrounding villages and forests. Mayan hunters caught rabbits, armadillos, iguanas, and deer for food. They also trapped brightly colored birds and fierce jaguars for their feathers and fur, which were used for ceremonial robes and headdresses. Mayan farmers burned areas of the forest to make clearings, where they grew crops of beans, maize, and squash.

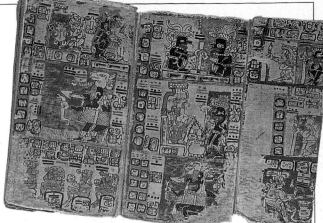

▲ *Mayan scribes kept records in folding books called codexes, which were made from thin strips of bark. These pages from a codex show Mayan gods and kings.*

GLYPHS—WRITING AND NUMBERS

The Maya were the first American civilization to keep written records. They developed a system of picture writing using "glyphs," with which they recorded the achievements of heroes and kings. The Maya were also skillful mathematicians, even though they used only three numbers—the glyph of a shell for zero, a dot for one, and a bar for five (*see right*). Mayan priests and astronomers worked out two very accurate calendars (one for the government and one for religious use) by making careful observations of the sun, moon, and stars.

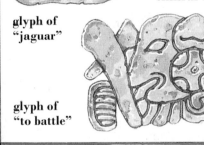

glyph of "jaguar"

glyph of "to battle"

glyph of "zero"

glyph of "one"

glyph of "five"

◀ *Human sacrifice played an important part in Mayan religious ceremonies. Prisoners captured in war were killed as offerings to the gods. The Maya believed that the captives' blood would feed the life-giving sun, make the rains fall, and encourage the crops to grow.*

▲ *This pottery figure shows a Mayan mother carrying her baby on her back. As soon as they were old enough, Mayan children were expected to help their parents in the fields and around the home.*

MEDIEVAL BAGHDAD

▶ From A.D. 732 to 1258, Muslim princes, called caliphs, ruled a large empire in north Africa and the Middle East. The caliphs' duties were to defend the Islamic faith and to protect and strengthen Muslim lands.

SPAIN

PRINCESS AMAT AL-AZIZ was born in about A.D. 758 into one of the most powerful families in the world. Her grandfather was Caliph al-Mansūr, magnificent ruler of the Muslim empire from A.D. 754 to A.D. 775. He called the princess Zubaidah, which means "butterball" in Arabic, because she was such a plump and cuddly baby. She used this name all her life.

Zubaidah lived in the royal palace in Baghdad. She could have anything she wanted. She liked jeweled slippers and clothes embroidered with gold. She had delicious food, including fruit cooled with ice brought by runners from faraway mountains.

Zubaidah married Prince Harun al-Rashid, who became caliph in A.D. 785. Zubaidah was wise, and the caliph valued her advice. She encouraged music and painting and paid for drinking-water fountains and rest houses along the pilgrim routes to the holy city of Mecca, in Arabia. One Baghdad poet wrote, "She had the deepest desire to do good."

◀ The caliphs' palaces were filled with the finest goods that local craftspeople could make. The pattern on this ninth-century dish was copied from rare Chinese pottery. The caliphs also had dishes made of gold and silver.

▲ Boys in Baghdad went to schools like this, or were taught by the preachers at their local mosque. Muslim scholars were especially skilled in medicine, math, astronomy (the study of the stars), and science.

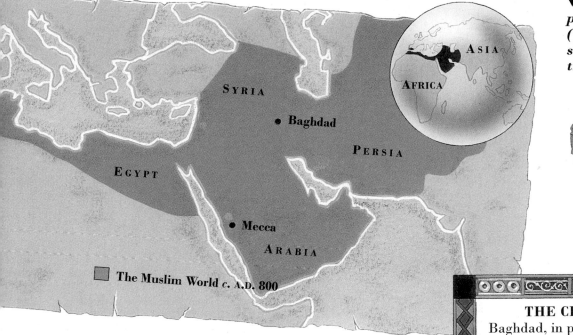

The Muslim World c. A.D. 800

▼ *Children living in Baghdad played games like La 'b al dabb ("the lizard game"), which was similar to today's game of pin the tail on the donkey.*

THE MUSLIM WORLD

By about A.D. 800, the Muslim world stretched from southern Spain into central Asia. Some Muslim lands were ruled by the caliph of Baghdad; others were ruled by local princes who had made special agreements with him.

Throughout the Muslim world, people followed the Muslim faith (called Islam), received a Muslim education, and followed Muslim laws. They paid taxes to the caliph. There were smaller groups of people of different faiths—mostly Christians and Jews—in many Muslim lands. They were treated fairly, but had to pay extra taxes and sometimes had to wear special clothes to show who they were.

◀ *As a child, Zubaidah spent her days in the luxurious women's quarters of the royal palace. There, she would read and write, sing and dance, listen to musicians and storytellers, and play with her brothers and sisters.*

THE CITY OF BAGHDAD

Baghdad, in present-day Iraq, was founded in A.D. 762 by Caliph al-Mansūr. Its name means "city of peace," and it became one of the biggest, richest, and most splendid cities in the world. It was built to a circular design (*below*), with the caliph's palace, the great mosque, and the royal gardens at its center. It included colleges, hospitals, and an observatory.

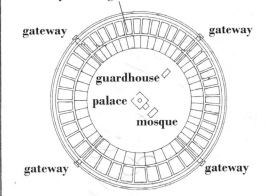

houses and government and army buildings

gateway   gateway

guardhouse

palace

mosque

gateway   gateway

The city of Baghdad was destroyed in 1258 (*see below*) by powerful armies of Mongol soldiers from central Asia.

THE VIKINGS

Egil as he may have looked

EGIL SKALLAGRIMSSON could run fast, fight bravely, sing, and make up poems. He was very clever, but he was also wild, disobedient, and rude. When Egil was six, he killed another boy in a rage while they were playing ball. His mother was proud of him: "A proper little Viking," she said. But Egil's father was furious. Three years later, Egil decided, "I want to be a Viking and go on Viking raids." He forced his older brother, Thorolf, to let him sail with him, and Egil spent many years on the seas, raiding, fighting—and writing poems.

Egil lived sometime between A.D. 1000 and A.D. 1100—toward the end of the Viking age—in the village of Borg in Iceland. The Icelandic poet Snorri Sturluson wrote a long poem (called a saga) about Egil's life. Some poets invented stories to put in their sagas to make them more exciting. But many historians think that most of what Sturluson wrote about Egil is true.

▼ *The Vikings lived in Norway, Denmark, and Sweden. From the late eighth century they settled in other parts of Europe. They set up trading towns in Russia and traveled to Constantinople (now Istanbul). Viking sailors discovered Iceland in A.D. 870, Greenland in A.D. 985, and landed in America in A.D. 1001.*

▼ *Egil sailed on his first voyage when he was only twelve years old. Usually Viking boys had to be at least sixteen years old before they were allowed to take part in such dangerous adventures. Many Viking warriors were killed or injured on raids.*

▼ *The Vikings enjoyed good food and drink and listening to songs and stories after a feast. They retold old stories and made up new poems praising explorers, heroes, and gods.*

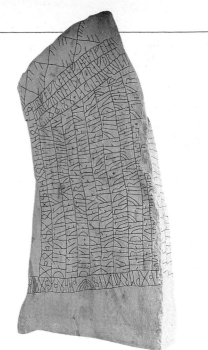

▲ *Viking children did not go to school. Instead they helped their parents in their fields or workshops or around the house. Girls also learned spinning and weaving.*

RAIDERS AND TRADERS

The Vikings were bold raiders and skillful sailors. Between A.D. 793 and A.D. 1100, they terrorized northern Europe, swooping across the sea in their long, sleek boats to bring death and destruction to churches and villages along the coast. But not all Vikings were bloodthirsty pirates. Many lived peacefully as fishermen and farmers, or as merchants and craftspeople in busy trading towns. The Vikings had a democratic system of government and laws. They also had a rich tradition of music, poetry, and storytelling, which was passed down through the generations by word of mouth.

▲ *The Vikings made beautiful stone monuments in memory of dead friends and relations. Often the stones were carved with a message in runes (the letters of the Viking alphabet). This stone was made for a dead son.*

SHIPS FOR LIFE AND DEATH

Strong, graceful wooden ships were central to the Vikings' way of life. The Vikings needed ships for trading, going on raids, and for sailing to new settlements in distant lands. Ships also played an important part in Viking funerals. Men and women were buried in worn-out ships sunk deep into the ground or inside boat-shaped rings of stones like the one in this photograph. The Vikings saw death as an exciting, but frightening, voyage into the unknown. They hoped that the ships in which they were buried would carry their spirits safely into the next world.

THE MONGOLS

Aiyaruk as she may have looked

AIYARUK was a Mongol princess, born in about 1265. Her name means "bright moon," and she was very beautiful.

When Aiyaruk was about fifteen years old, her father arranged for her to marry a fine young prince from another Mongol tribe. But Aiyaruk would not agree. She was strong, brave, and a superb rider. She had learned all the Mongol warrior skills, such as how to fight on horseback and how to shoot a moving target. So Aiyaruk decided that she would only marry a man who was stronger and braver than she was.

Many bold young warriors came to fight against Aiyaruk. She defeated them all. Aiyaruk never married, but lived her life as a soldier. She became a famous general and led her father's army to war.

This story was told by the explorer Marco Polo, who said that he had heard it from Mongol men and women he met on his travels. We do not know for certain whether it is true but many Mongol women did learn to ride and fight in wars. A few became famous war leaders.

▼ The Mongols came from the plains to the north and northwest of China. Under Genghis Khan, who became their leader in 1206, they conquered a vast empire. After Genghis Khan's death in 1227 the empire was divided into four states and extended into China.

ASIA
AFRICA

(RUSSIA)
Khanate of the Golden Horde
Chagatai Khanate
Il-Khan Empire

⬛ Mongol Empire c. 1279

▼ Aiyaruk fought on horseback, like all Mongol soldiers. They could shoot arrows to kill their enemies while riding at a gallop. They used four types of arrows to shoot long distances, pierce metal armor, set fire to enemy camps, or to send signals by making a whistling noise.

◀ The Italian explorer Marco Polo (1254–1324) wrote down the story of Aiyaruk's life. He spent many years traveling in China, India, and the Mongol lands and visited the court of Kublai Khan, the grandson of Genghis Khan. Polo wrote a book about his travels, which we can still read today.

NOMAD WARRIORS

The Mongols were nomads. They had no settled homes and did not grow any crops. Instead, they moved from place to place, hunting wild animals for food and seeking fresh grass for their horses, sheep, and cows. Everyone traveled on horseback—Mongol children were taught to ride by the time they were five years old.

Mongol men and women valued warrior skills, such as toughness, bravery, and strength. Rival tribes often fought one another, and other nations nearby. The Mongols were fearsome enemies—bold, bloodthirsty, and cruel. They killed all who fought against them. But they spared anyone who surrendered immediately.

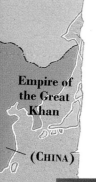

Empire of the Great Khan

(CHINA)

◀ *We know what the Mongols were like from stories and pictures created by people who fought against them, such as the Persians and Chinese. This Mongol warrior on his horse was painted by a Chinese artist in the thirteenth century. The soldier is well armed with a bow and a quiver full of arrows.*

▼ *Mongol armies made gruesome "towers of skulls" like this one, shown in a sixteenth-century painting. They cut off their conquered enemies' heads and arranged them in a tall heap, supported by bricks or stones. As the heads rotted, the tower of skulls gave off a faint, ghostly light.*

MOVABLE HOMES

Mongol families lived in big tents called yurts or gers, which were made of thick woolen cloth stretched over a wooden frame. In summer, the Mongols pitched their yurts on the high steppes (flat grasslands) that stretched across central Asia from China to Russia. In winter, they camped in river valleys to shelter from the bitterly cold winds from the North Pole. When they moved, the yurts were collapsed and lifted onto huge carts pulled by oxen.

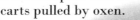

CHINA AND THE SILK ROAD

A Chinese boy from a fourteenth-century scroll

THE YOUNG BOY pictured on the left was painted by a Chinese artist in about A.D. 1300. We do not know the boy's name, but we can guess what his life was like from what we know about people living in China at the time. He lived in a big city. It was crowded and full of life, and was governed by lots of laws. Some of these laws were designed to prevent crimes like theft from shops; others, such as fire regulations or street-cleaning schemes, protected people's safety and health.

The boy's home was comfortable, but crowded with members of his family. He washed in the public bathhouse and, when he wasn't working, he took boat trips down the river or played in the city's parks. His family could buy a great variety of cheap, fresh food in the city's markets, and they wore silk robes. His father was probably a craftsman or merchant, who was already training his son for the same career. Chinese cities had grown rich through trade, and merchants and craftspeople were highly respected for their skills.

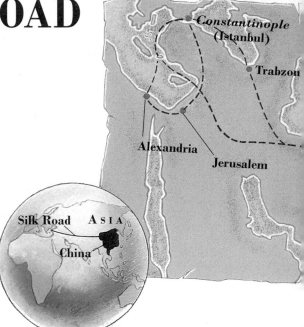

▲ Valuable goods made in China were carried long distances overland to Europe along the "Silk Road." This was not a single roadway, but a series of paths used by merchants from many lands. Along the way, they rested and traded at busy market towns.

▶ The city of Kaifeng was the capital of southern China during the eleventh and twelfth centuries. It was a great center of trade and manufacturing. It had a busy harbor, shopping malls, craft workshops, restaurants, and tea gardens.

CHINA UNDER THE SONG DYNASTY

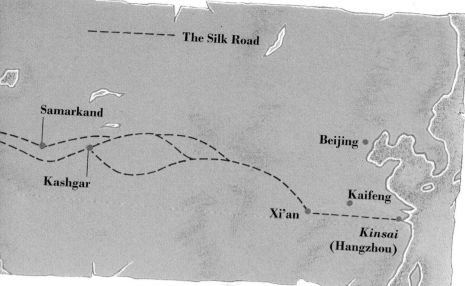

The Silk Road

Samarkand

Kashgar

Beijing

Kaifeng

Xi'an

Kinsai
(Hangzhou)

The Song dynasty (dynasty means "ruling family") came to power in A.D. 960, after fifty years of civil war. It brought three centuries of peace for most people living in China, and the population grew rapidly. In A.D. 750, the population of China was about 60 million, but by A.D. 1100 it had reached more than 110 million.

More food was needed to feed all these people, so Chinese scientists developed new varieties of rice which gave bigger harvests, and engineered vast schemes to channel water to the crops.

There were changes in Chinese society, too. In the past, old noble families had run the government. Now, clever students from ordinary families could compete for government jobs. Many new schools were set up, and the Chinese invented lots of useful and amazing things, such as ships' rudders and kites.

▼ *Traveling peddlers walked through the city streets selling trinkets, household goods, and toys. This fan, showing a mother buying toys for her children from a peddler, was painted in about A.D. 1200.*

▶ *Silk cloth and porcelain (a very fine, delicate pottery) were both Chinese inventions. Silk was already being made by 1500 B.C.; porcelain was not invented until the Song dynasty.*

FAMILY LIFE

Families were very important to Chinese people. Parents, children, grandparents, uncles, and aunts all lived in the same house, worked together, and shared the family meal. All the members of a family had a duty to help one another, whether they were living or dead. Living people prayed to their dead ancestors, hoping to receive guidance. They also gave offerings to their ancestors' spirits at family altars to help the spirits survive.

THE CHILDREN'S CRUSADE

STEPHEN WAS A SHEPHERD BOY from the village of Cloyes in northern France. He was deeply religious, and he lived in a time when there were lots of powerful and exciting religious ideas. One day in 1212, Stephen met a pilgrim who gave him "a letter from heaven." The pilgrim told Stephen to take the letter to the king of France and tell him to join the Crusades (*see page 27*). Stephen and his friends decided to make the long walk to Paris and give the letter to the king. Many other children joined them. They hoped the king would lead them on a crusade to the Holy Land. But the king refused. Some medieval writers say that Stephen and the children set off by themselves to walk to the Holy Land. Others say they were robbed and killed on the long journey back home to Cloyes.

Later that same year, a boy called Nicholas led children on a crusade from Germany. But their adventure ended in tragedy, too. They managed to reach Italy, but they were robbed, killed, or sold as slaves.

▶ The French children's crusade reached no farther than Paris. The German children traveled as far as seaports in Italy and France. None of them reached the Holy Land.

▲ Children from ordinary families were expected to help around the house and to work in the fields. This little girl is helping her mother to cook by keeping the fire going with bellows.

▲ Young children from noble families were sometimes sent to monasteries to become monks or nuns. The children's prayers were believed to bring their families closer to God.

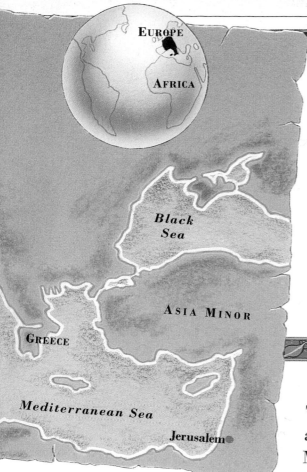

CHRISTIAN KNIGHTS

Knights were soldiers who fought on horseback. Usually they came from noble families and had the right to be called "Sir." They helped kings and princes defend their lands. The Church taught that it was also a knight's duty to protect the Christian faith.

It was very expensive to become a knight. A warhorse, a suit of armor, and good swords cost a lot of money. Only nobles and well-paid professional soldiers could afford all this equipment, so men from ordinary families fought on foot. They wore simple armor made of padded leather, and they fought with pikes, long sticks, and bows and arrows.

HOLY WARS

The Crusades were a series of wars fought between Christian and Muslim armies between 1096 and 1291. Christians and Muslims quarreled over who had the right to rule the Holy Land—the city of Jerusalem and the surrounding area (in present-day Israel and nearby). Soldiers from all over Christian Europe and from Muslim countries in North Africa and the Middle East believed it was their religious duty to leave their families and go to fight in the Crusades. Many traveled long distances, and most of them never returned home. They were killed in battle or died from disease. Muslim soldiers finally drove the Christians out of the Holy Land in 1291.

▼ *Crowds of children followed Stephen to Paris to see the king. They carried crosses and candles and chanted prayers. But the king refused to join their crusade. He told them to be good and go home.*

▲ *Boys began training to be knights when they were seven or eight years old. They learned how to ride horses, studied battle plans, and practiced fighting with swords made of wood. They did not become real knights until they were about twenty-one years old.*

CLOTHES

PEOPLE WEAR CLOTHES FOR ALL SORTS of reasons. In cold climates, clothes keep us warm. In hot lands, they protect us from the sun's rays and help to keep us cool.

Clothes can tell us a lot about people, now and in the past. For example, the cloaks, tunics, and headdresses worn by wealthy Aztec people were decorated with embroidery and jewel-colored feathers from tropical birds. Costly clothes like these displayed wealth and rank, and showed that the wearer did not have to do hard, dirty work like farming or cleaning.

Before the nineteenth century there were no factories and big machines producing huge quantities of fabrics and clothing. And man-made fabrics like nylon were not invented until the twentieth century. In the past, clothes were made from the materials that were available in the places people lived. Animal skins were colored with dyes made from plants and earth. Wool and cotton were woven and sewn into clothes by hand, usually by women for their families. They used other natural materials, such as teeth, bones, seeds, and even fish scales, for decoration.

◀ *In the icy Arctic, mothers carried their babies inside the cozy, fur-lined hoods of their sealskin jackets (which they called parkas or anoraks). This Inuit mother and her baby were painted in North America in 1585.*

▶ *Aztec children in the sixteenth century dressed similarly to adults. Men and boys wore loincloths and cloaks fastened at the shoulder. Women and girls wore tunic tops and long skirts. The richness of decoration on clothing showed how wealthy and important the wearer was. Boys had to wear their hair loose until they had killed someone in battle.*

▼ This advertisement appeared in newspapers in nineteenth-century England. It shows a mother and her daughter wearing corsets to give them fashionably small waists. But very tight corsets could damage a woman's ribs, stomach, and liver, and cause pain and disease.

◀ Children from wealthy families in sixteenth-century Europe were dressed like their parents. Rich silks and lace displayed their families' rank. Boys as well as girls wore skirts until they were about five years old. Then boys wore trousers.

▶ These girls are from the Ge people in southern China. Traditionally, Ge girls were expected to be able to sew beautifully. They learned to sew from about age eight. On special occasions, they wore traditional costumes, which they had made themselves over many years to show off their skill.

▼ For centuries, girls of the Mbuti people of Zaire in Africa have worn special clothes and painted their bodies to take part in traditional dances.

▼ Boys and girls living in northern Australia wore hardly any clothes because the weather is very hot. Boys were given a necklace of fur tassels when they grew up as a sign that they had become men.

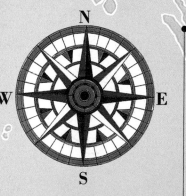

▶ In some countries, religious laws and customs have laid down rules for the clothes that girls and boys should wear. These Muslim girls come from Malaysia.

RENAISSANCE GERMANY

Dürer drew this portrait of himself in 1484, when he was thirteen years old

ALBRECHT DÜRER was born in 1471 in southern Germany. His father was a famous goldsmith and he wanted Albrecht to become a goldsmith, too. He sent Albrecht to school to learn to read and write, then took him into his own workshop and began to teach his son all the skills of a goldsmith.

But Albrecht was not happy. He wanted to be a painter. He made many beautiful drawings to prove to his father that he could be successful. Finally his father agreed, and in 1486 Albrecht went to study with Michael Wolgemut, one of Nuremberg's best-known painters.

Albrecht worked hard and learned quickly. While he was still only a teenager his drawings were carved onto wooden blocks and printed for sale in many European lands. He became one of the greatest German artists in history.

▼ *Dürer lived in Nuremberg, in Germany, at the height of the Renaissance (see page 31). Beginning in Italy in about 1400, the Renaissance quickly spread across Europe, encouraged by the wealth brought by trade.*

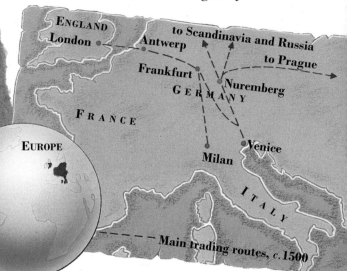

ENGLAND
London
Antwerp
to Scandinavia and Russia
to Prague
Frankfurt
Nuremberg
GERMANY
FRANCE
EUROPE
Milan
Venice
ITALY
Main trading routes, c.1500

▼ *As a child, Albrecht Dürer often visited the workshop of his godfather, Anton Koberger, who was a printer. Individual letters of type were arranged into pages of text, which were coated with ink ready to be used on the huge press. Printed sheets of paper were hung up to dry.*

▲ *Girls from craft-worker families were often taught at home by their mothers to read and write. A few also learned craft skills.*

THE CITY OF NUREMBERG

Nuremberg was a very wealthy city. It lay close to long-distance trading routes linking Italy and northern Europe (*see map on page 30*). There were also rich iron and silver mines nearby.

Bankers, merchants, artists, scholars, printers, and expert craftspeople lived in Nuremberg. The city's craftspeople were especially skilled at metalwork. They were famous throughout Europe for making elaborate gold and silver dishes, fine guns, swords, and beautifully decorated suits of armor, locks, and accurate navigation instruments.

Nuremberg's citizens were rich, well educated, and proud. They paid for big houses and fine churches. The whole city was protected by a strong wall.

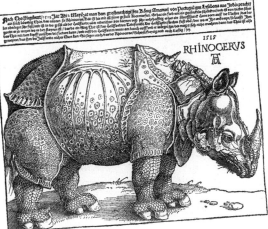

◀ *Some of the first printed books used woodblocks. The carved image, such as this rhinoceros by Dürer, was covered with ink. Sheets of paper were then pressed down on top of it and lifted off.*

THE RENAISSANCE

Dürer lived during the Renaissance—a time of exciting new ideas in art, architecture, and learning. In the Renaissance, which means "rebirth," many artists, writers, and scholars invented new styles and tried new techniques. They rediscovered ancient Greek and Roman knowledge, which had been lost for hundreds of years, and they began looking at the world in a more scientific way.

Dürer's drawings are typical of the time. They show people, animals, and plants in a very lifelike way, and were based on scientific study.

Renaissance ideas were spread by printing. The first book to be printed in Europe was produced in 1445. Before that, single copies of books were carefully handwritten. Now, many copies of books could be made more quickly and cheaply.

Dürer used printing to make copies of his own work.

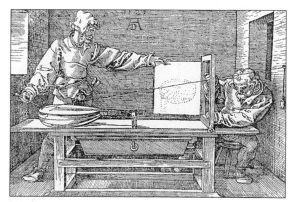

▲ *Like many Renaissance artists, Dürer was interested in the way our eyes see things. He designed this frame to help artists make their drawings more lifelike.*

BENIN

PRINCE OGUN was the son of the Oba, or king, of Benin. When his father died in about 1420, Ogun should have been the next Oba. But many people plotted against him, including his older brother. They drove Ogun out of Benin City. He lived secretly in the forest for twenty years. Then Ogun's older brother died. Ogun's younger brother became the next Oba because everyone thought that Ogun had been killed long ago by wild animals in the forest. But Ogun was not dead. He left the forest and made his way to Benin City where he hid until he had a chance to take power himself.

Prince Ogun defeated his brother and became Oba in 1440. He ruled until 1473. Ogun took a new name, Ewuare, which means "trouble is over." Under his leadership, Benin grew rich and powerful. He reorganized the government and conquered two hundred towns and villages. He became known as "Ewuare the Great."

▼ The kingdom of Benin was in west Africa, in the south of the present-day nation of Nigeria. Benin was one of the strongest of a number of powerful kingdoms that flourished in Africa from the thirteenth century.

AFRICA

Kanem-Borno
Songhay and Mali
Mamluk Egypt
Akan Ife Benin
Funj
Kongo
Zimbabwe

☐ Powerful African kingdoms c. 1200–1600 (includes Benin)

▼ As a young boy, Prince Ogun watched his father, the Oba, take part in special festivals escorted by warriors and musicians. Great parades through the streets and outside the royal palace displayed the Oba's royal power.

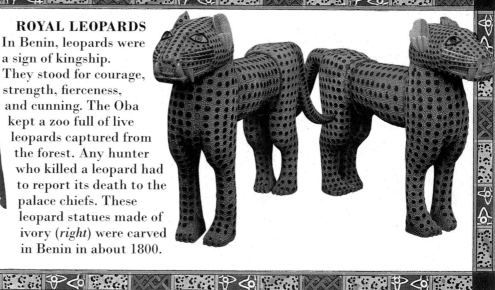

ROYAL LEOPARDS
In Benin, leopards were a sign of kingship. They stood for courage, strength, fierceness, and cunning. The Oba kept a zoo full of live leopards captured from the forest. Any hunter who killed a leopard had to report its death to the palace chiefs. These leopard statues made of ivory (*right*) were carved in Benin in about 1800.

▲ *This bronze plaque shows the Oba Ohen who ruled some time between 1300 and 1350. Some legends say that, late in his life, Oba Ohen's legs became paralyzed. The artist has shown this by making the Oba's feet look like floppy fish. But the two leopards Ohen is holding remind everyone that he still has royal power.*

◀ *Houses in Benin were built of red, sun-baked mud, with roofs of dried reeds and grass. After every storm, children had to bring mud from the riverbank and spread it over the walls of the houses to repair the damage caused by the heavy rain.*

BUILDING A KINGDOM

The kingdom of Benin first became powerful between A.D. 900 and A.D. 1200. Farming was the main way of life, and the people of Benin cleared fields in the rain forest where they grew crops such as yams for food. Huge earthworks of banks and ditches were built to defend the fields and villages from attack. As the kingdom grew more powerful, the capital city, also called Benin, began to grow. By 1550 Benin was the richest and strongest state in Africa.

Many Obas encouraged trade and craftwork. After about 1280, a guild of specially trained bronze casters began to make beautiful statues and plaques like the one above. The people of Benin did not have a system of writing, but they kept records of important people and events on these plaques.

▲ *Children took part in a festival to bring happiness to their families. Early in the morning, they went into the forest carrying burning sticks to drive away evil spirits. They returned home with armfuls of fresh leaves, which they called "leaves of joy."*

THE INCAS

ONCE A YEAR government officials from the Inca's royal palace set out to choose the prettiest, best-behaved girls from each of the surrounding villages. The girls would become "Maidens of the Sun." They and their families could not refuse—but it was a great honor to be chosen.

The girls were taken from their villages at the age of nine or ten and sent to a special school. There, wise, holy women tutors called *Mamacunas* taught the girls about religion and showed them how to weave fine clothes for the Inca to wear. When the Maidens of the Sun were about thirteen years old, they were taken to meet the Inca himself.

He chose some of the girls to be his servants and some to be his wives. He sent others to help the priests in the temples, or to train as Mamacunas. Lastly, he chose a few to be killed as a special offering to the gods.

▶ The Incas' capital city of Cuzco—the "Sacred City of the Sun"—was built high up in the Andes Mountains. These walls formed part of the city's fortress, called Sacsahuaman.

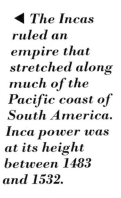

SOUTH AMERICA

Atlantic Ocean

SOUTH AMERICA

Cuzco

THE INCA EMPIRE c. 1525

Pacific Ocean

◀ The Incas ruled an empire that stretched along much of the Pacific coast of South America. Inca power was at its height between 1483 and 1532.

▼ Inca Maidens of the Sun made beautiful clothes for members of the royal family and important government officials. This poncho (worn like a loose tunic) is decorated with patterns of flowers and cats.

◀▶ In 1995, the body of an Inca girl was found frozen in the ice at the top of Mount Ampato in Peru. She was dressed in beautiful clothes (see left), with a headdress of feathers. She was probably left there five hundred years ago as a sacrifice to the mountain-god. Offerings of maize, pottery, llamas, and little statues (right) were found nearby.

THE INCA EMPIRE

The Quechua people lived in the Andes Mountains. By about 1200, the Quechua had become a strong nation ruled by kings called Incas—the "Sons of the Sun." In 1438, Inca Pachacuti started to build up a vast empire by conquering neighboring lands. Men and women ruled by the Incas were given work by government officials—they might be chosen as priests, soldiers, farmers, craftspeople, messengers, or slaves. The government also gave them rations of food and clothes. Inca kings collected taxes from conquered peoples and became very rich. They built an amazing network of roads through their empire. But Inca power collapsed after Spanish explorers invaded Inca lands in 1532.

CHILDREN'S LIVES

Children living in the Inca empire worked hard. They were given different jobs to do depending on how old they were, and whether they were boys or girls. At nine years old, boys (*above left*) chased birds away from crops, caught birds, and collected colorful feathers for Inca headdresses. Girls aged nine looked after animals, picked cotton (*above right*), and learned spinning and weaving. Babies were well cared for. To keep them safe, they were strapped inside cradles (*top right*) for their first year.

◀ *In their convent in the city of Cuzco, the Maidens of the Sun spun fine thread from the hair of the alpaca (an animal related to the llama). They dyed the thread, using plants and crushed earth, and wove it into complicated patterns on back-strap looms.*

SHAKESPEARE'S ENGLAND

▼ *Shakespeare was born in Stratford-upon-Avon, but went in search of fame and fortune in London, with its fine theaters and actors.*

AT THE AGE OF TWELVE, Nathan Field was already acting leading roles on the stage in front of Queen Elizabeth I. Born in 1587, he became a very famous boy actor. The names of most boy actors of the time have long been forgotten, but we do know a little about Nathan. It seems likely that he played the parts of some important female characters in Shakespeare's plays. At that time, women did not act on the stage. It was not "respectable"—and few men believed that women would be able to remember their lines. So all women's parts were acted by specially trained boys like Nathan. He was so successful as an actor that famous writers, like Ben Jonson, created parts especially for him. When Field grew up, he continued to work in the theater. He wrote comic plays and acted in them. He died in 1620, at the age of thirty-three.

Nathan Field playing a female role on stage in the sixteenth century

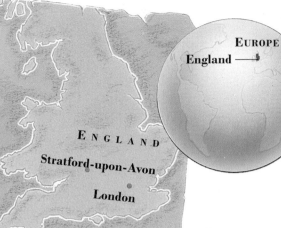

▼ *The fairies and their Queen in Shakespeare's play, A Midsummer Night's Dream, were played by boy actors like Nathan Field. On stage he wore wigs, makeup, padding, and sometimes high-heeled shoes.*

WILLIAM SHAKESPEARE

Although William Shakespeare lived from 1564 to 1616—some four hundred years ago—he is famous today as England's greatest dramatist. After starting out as an actor in London, he wrote more than forty plays. Some, such as *A Midsummer Night's Dream*, are comedies, full of jokes. Some, like *Henry V*, are dramatic re-tellings of historical events. Others, like *Hamlet*, are tragedies, which are full of death and disaster, but are very exciting to watch. Shakespeare also wrote many great poems, including *The Sonnets*.

▲ *Young children learned to read using "hornbooks" like this. A printed sheet of paper was pasted on a wooden board and covered with a thin, transparent sheet of cow's horn. The handle made the book easy to hold.*

QUEEN ELIZABETH I

For most of Shakespeare's life, Queen Elizabeth I ruled England. When she first came to power, in 1558, the royal family was unpopular. England was not a wealthy country, and its government was weak. The English people were also divided by bitter quarrels about religion. No one welcomed Elizabeth as queen or thought that a woman would be able to rule their country.

But Elizabeth proved them wrong. She passed strict laws to settle the religious quarrels and made peace with dangerous enemies. She encouraged trade and increased England's power abroad. In 1588, English troops defeated the attacking Spanish battle-fleet (called the Armada). Elizabeth was brave, strong-minded, cunning, and sometimes cruel, but she became very popular. She enjoyed watching plays, and many of Shakespeare's works were performed for the first time at her royal court. After her death in 1603, people looked back on her reign as a golden age, and called her "Good Queen Bess."

▶ *By about 1600, there were "grammar schools" in most big towns. Lessons started at 7 A.M. and finished at 5 P.M., although children had two hours off in the middle of the day. Teachers were very strict. Boys were caned if they made mistakes in their work or misbehaved.*

▲ *Girls and boys from rich, noble families were often educated at home by private tutors. Girls also had to learn to run a large house and entertain important guests. The elaborate clothes they wore (above) displayed the wealth and rank of their family.*

MAYFLOWER PILGRIMS

▼ *The Pilgrims set sail from Plymouth, in southwest England. After more than two months at sea, they reached the shores of Massachusetts, on the northeast American coast.*

MARY ALLERTON was only nine years old when she sailed from England with her parents, in September 1620. They and many other passengers were traveling across the Atlantic Ocean to a new life in America.

They had a long and terrible journey in a small, cramped ship called the *Mayflower*. They planned to build a new community in Virginia with other families who had already settled there. But the *Mayflower* was blown off course northward by strong winds and huge waves. Some time later, one of the passengers wrote about the journey: "After a long beating at sea, they fell with that land which is called Cape Cod . . . they were not a little joyfull." This was on November 19. But the weather was still wild, and the winter snow had come, so the travelers could not land. For more than a month, Mary and the other passengers had to stay on board the miserably cold and damp ship. At last, on December 26, the weather was calm enough for them to row across to the shore of their new land.

▼ *It was bitterly cold when Mary Allerton was at last rowed ashore from the Mayflower. The weather was so bad that the Pilgrims were unable to start building shelters straightaway. Instead, they had to return to the ship and camp on board until the weather grew warmer.*

NORTH AMERICA   EUROPE

NORTH AMERICA

Atlantic Ocean

Plymouth, Massachusetts

VIRGINIA

◀ *The Pilgrims landed in America just as a terrible winter began. More than half of them died from hunger and cold. The survivors built houses from wood as soon as they were able. They named their new village "Plymouth," after the port they had sailed from.*

A NEW WAY OF LIFE

In sixteenth-century England, many people quarreled—and fought—about religion. So the government passed laws to make everyone stop fighting, and worship in the same way. By 1608, a small group of families decided they could no longer obey these laws. They wanted to be able to choose for themselves how to worship, and to follow a simple, religious way of life.

They left England and went to the Netherlands, but ran short of money and did not feel happy there. In 1620, they decided to emigrate to America and set up a new community. In America, they would be free to run their own church and to worship in the way they believed was right. They would make their own laws, which they based on the Bible.

The *Mayflower* passengers did not call themselves "Pilgrims." They were first referred to as the Pilgrim Fathers in 1799, and the name has been used to describe them ever since.

▲ *Friendly Native Americans showed the Pilgrims how to grow maize and catch fish for food. The Pilgrims had brought seeds of food plants from England, but they would not grow in America. These Native Americans are eating a meal of succotash (maize and beans).*

deck

captain's cabin

below deck, where most Pilgrims sheltered

food and water stores

THE *MAYFLOWER*

For their journey, the Pilgrims bought a second-hand merchant ship called the *Mayflower*. Built in the early seventeenth century, the *Mayflower* was made of wood. It had been built as a cargo ship for transporting wine, and it was not designed to carry passengers. It was very small—only 90 feet long and 26 feet wide. The 102 Pilgrims and their crew, together with food, water, and clothes for the journey, and seeds and farm equipment for the new land, spent weeks crammed into this tiny space.

THE FRENCH REVOLUTION

MARIE-VICTOIRE MONNARD was the oldest of fifteen children from a working-class family living in France. She was eleven years old when the Revolution began in 1789. Years later, she wrote about what happened. She described how angry peasants rampaged through her village, desperate for food, while she and her sisters were shut in the hayloft—the safest place their mother could find to hide them.

By 1792, Marie-Victoire had moved to Paris and, at the age of thirteen, had found work as a trainee dressmaker. She heard the cries as hundreds of supporters of the French royal family were killed by angry mobs. She remembered "shaking with terror." But, she said, "We went on working, just like any other day." Things got worse in 1793. Day after day, Marie-Victoire saw carts loaded with men and women on their way to the guillotine. They had been accused of being against the Revolution, and were sentenced to death. Later, carts full of headless bodies dripping with blood rumbled back through the city streets.

▼ Riots against the king and the government broke out across France in 1789. By 1793–94, the leaders of the Revolution were calling for the execution of many thousands of people.

EUROPE
France

Areas of mass executions, 1793–94

Arras

Paris

Areas of rioting, 1789

Angers

Nantes

Lyons

Bordeaux

Orange

border of France, 1793

Toulon

Marseilles

◄ Queen Marie-Antoinette of France was executed in 1793 by supporters of the Revolution, but her children were allowed to survive.

WHY DID IT HAPPEN?

The French Revolution began in 1789 as a series of protests. Ordinary people complained about poverty, heavy taxes, and shortages of food. Merchants and manufacturers criticized the government's handling of the country's economy. Almost everyone complained about the royal family: the king and his advisors were weak; the queen was extravagant—and a foreigner, too.

The protests turned into bloodshed, and during six terrible years, the leaders of the Revolution had thousands of people killed using a new machine—the guillotine. The king and queen, priests, and anyone who did not agree with the Revolution were executed.

But the leaders quarreled among themselves and they, too, were executed, bringing the Revolution to an end in 1795.

▲ *Families cheered the National Guard, which was set up to defend France against enemies of the Revolution. Ordinary people believed that the Revolution would create a better world for them. But most stayed just as poor.*

▲ *By 1793, no one dared go out without a red-white-and-blue cockade (badge) in their hat to show that they supported the Revolution. If they forgot their cockade, they might be executed, too. About three thousand people were guillotined in Paris in one year.*

RICH AND POOR

Before and after the Revolution, children from poor families faced hunger and hard work (*below right*). They had little chance of going to school or of training for well-paid jobs. Like their parents, they could only get low-paid jobs as servants, peasant farmers, or unskilled laborers.

Children from wealthy families (*above*) received a good education. They studied—and played—until they were at least sixteen years old. Boys learned how to run their families' estates, or trained for moneymaking careers. Girls were taught how to manage a large household, and how to find a suitable husband. For them, marriage was the only acceptable career.

CHILDREN AT WORK

FROM ANCIENT TIMES, CHILDREN FROM ordinary families across the world have had to work to help their families survive. Few countries offered free schooling, and only wealthy parents could afford to give their children a good education. They paid for classes or private tutors for their children, who were brought up to continue the family's status. Boys were trained to take professional jobs or to manage the family's estate. Girls learned how to run a large household.

Children from ordinary families, however, worked hard alongside their parents in the fields or in the home. Many families needed the small amount of money their children could earn if they worked. Some boys and girls were sent away from their families to be servants in the houses of wealthy people. Other children, often as young as eight years old, worked in terrible conditions in factories.

As children worked, they learned the skills that would help them earn a living when they were grown up. But without an education, they had very little chance of getting a professional qualification, or an interesting, well-paid job such as in medicine or law.

▼ These Native American girls from about 1830 are scraping fat and hair from buffalo skins. They lived in the Great Plains region of the United States of America. Cleaning skins before using them to make clothes and tepees (tents) was women's work, along with cooking, cleaning, and childcare.

▶ Most sugar plantations, like this one in Antigua in about 1823, were worked by slaves. The slaves belonged to their owners and were not allowed to leave the estates. Children who were born to slave parents were forced to become slaves and work alongside their families.

▶ *This young girl from India is spinning cotton thread by hand on a simple spinning wheel. She is working in a cool, shady courtyard outside her house, while friends and neighbors look on. This photograph was taken in the early 1900s.*

▼ *In many parts of Europe, girls from ordinary families were sent away from home when they were about twelve years old to work as servants in rich households. This nineteenth-century servant girl worked long hours cleaning, carrying coal for fires, peeling vegetables, and running errands.*

◀ *At the age of eight, boys from important families in medieval Europe were sent to live in other powerful households. They worked as pages and were expected to wait at the table, run errands, and sometimes help a knight look after his weapons, armor, and warhorses.*

▼ *This nineteenth-century wooden statue shows two women and a young girl from west Africa pounding millet to make flour. Girls were trained by helping their mothers in the home.*

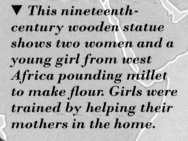

◀ *Children from farming families in ancient Greece were expected to help in the farmyard and fields. A boy on this Greek vase from about 520 B.C. is helping to harvest olives by climbing into the trees and shaking the fruit down.*

NATIVE AMERICANS

Mistippee aged about twelve, painted when in Washington in 1826

MISTIPPEE was the son of Yoholo-Micco, chief of the Creek Native people from southeast America. Mistippee was born in 1813. Like other Creek boys, he learned to hunt and fish, catch birds, and shoot with blowpipes and bows and arrows. He helped his parents dig their fields and plant seeds of maize, beans, and squash. When he was not working, he liked to sing and dance and play with the other boys in the village. They played lacrosse and a throwing game called "chunkey," which used wooden spears and a polished stone target.

Unusually, Mistippee also learned European skills, like reading and writing. This was because his father admired the ideas of Europeans living in America. He believed that these people could help Native Americans by providing them with better education and medical care. In 1826, Mistippee traveled with his father to meet important officials in Washington D.C., the capital city of the United States. Mistippee made a good impression on everyone he met.

▲ *Chinook mothers kept their babies safe in wooden carriers. A flattened forehead was a sign of high rank so mothers tied a piece of wood across their babies' heads to gently flatten their soft bones.*

NORTH AMERICA

Chinook
Bannock
Sioux
Wyandot
Washington D.C.
Creek

▲ *The Native American peoples mentioned on these pages lived in the areas shown on this map. During the 1800s, the United States government forced all native peoples to move to new areas where the government had decided they must live.*

▶ *Mistippee's people called lacrosse "Little Brother of War." Kicking, hitting, and trampling were all allowed and players could be badly injured. Top players were famous. They painted their bodies and wore a bead belt and a tail of horsehair.*

44

▶ *Sioux fathers taught their sons how to hunt and fight, and made small bows and arrows for them to practice with. After a boy's first kill, his father might hold a special feast to celebrate and might also give his son a new name.*

▲ *Bannock families lived in shelters made from branches covered with animal skins. Children learned to hunt rabbits and gather grubs, seeds, and nuts for food when they were very young.*

THE CREEK PEOPLE

The Creek, Chinook, Sioux, and Bannock peoples were among about three hundred different native peoples living in North America when the first European settlers arrived in the 1560s. Each group spoke its own language and made its own laws.

The way they lived depended on where their homeland was. The Creek people lived in the warm, wet southeast. They built large, carefully planned villages with houses made of wood and thatch. They were skilled in the use of herbal medicines, including tobacco and aspirin, which they prepared from the bark of trees.

Creek society was well organized, with strong leaders and laws. But sometimes there were bitter quarrels between those Creek people who admired the Europeans and those who hated them.

PEACE OR WAR?

Sometimes Native American peoples and European settlers managed to live peacefully side by side. This silver medal (*right*) was made to honor a friendly agreement of 1796 between the United States government and the Wyandot people, who lived in the state of Ohio.

But, at other times, there were quarrels between Native Americans and settlers, which often led to war. In 1830 the United States government decided that the Native Americans in the southeast should move from their homes so that settlers could live there instead. Many Native Americans fought against this, but they were forced to go. Some fell ill and died on the long miserable journey to "Indian Territory." This journey became known as the Trail of Tears.

GEORGE WASHINGTON
PRESIDENT 1793

AUSTRALIA

BALLANDELLA was an Aboriginal girl. She was born in 1832 in southern Australia. When she was little, her mother would carry Ballandella on her shoulders when she was too tired to walk, and caught snakes and lizards for them to eat. They were Ballandella's favorite food.

In 1836, Ballandella and her mother met a group of English explorers, led by the artist Thomas Mitchell. They decided to stay with the explorers for a while. Over the next six months Ballandella learned to speak English and to eat English food. She began to forget her old Aboriginal skills and way of life.

When her mother said that it was time to go back to their old home, Ballandella burst into tears. Her mother did not know what to do. She wanted her daughter to be happy. Eventually, she let Ballandella stay with the explorers. So Ballandella went to live with Thomas Mitchell and his wife. They brought her up with their own children. She was lively, cheerful, and did very well at school.

Ballandella age four, with her mother, drawn by Thomas Mitchell

▼ *Aboriginal families set up camp each night. They sat around the fire listening to wise old people singing songs and telling stories. The stories were often about the "Dreamtime"—long ago, when the Earth was created by the ancestors of all living creatures.*

▼ *This Aboriginal painting on tree bark shows a hunter (top) killing a kangaroo. Aboriginal artists sometimes drew the inside as well as the outside of people and animals—this picture shows the kangaroo's heart and spine. Aboriginal artists also drew pictures in sand and painted them on rocks and in caves.*

◄ *Aboriginal people have lived in Australia for at least 50,000 years. The first European settlement in Australia was set up little more than two hundred years ago, in 1788, at Botany Bay. By 1860, more than 900,000 European settlers had gone to live in Australia.*

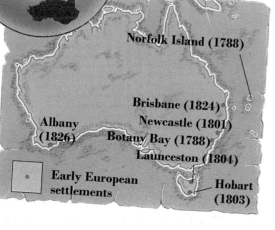

ASIA

AUSTRALIA

Norfolk Island (1788)

Brisbane (1824)

Albany (1826)

Newcastle (1801)

Botany Bay (1788)

Launceston (1804)

 Early European settlements

Hobart (1803)

AN ANCIENT WAY OF LIFE

Over the centuries, Aboriginal people developed skills that allowed them to survive in a harsh but beautiful land. Aboriginal hunters (usually men) tracked and speared animals, harpooned fish, trapped eels, snakes, and lizards, and caught birds in nets. They dived for turtles and shellfish and climbed trees to collect birds' eggs. Aboriginal women used digging sticks to collect roots and grubs for food, and learned how to make poisonous palm-tree fruits safe to eat.

Most Aboriginal people lived as nomads, moving from camp to camp and following ancient paths in search of food. Everyone learned where they would find the best food at different times of the year. They also learned how to find water in the desert and to make fire by rubbing dry twigs together. They sometimes started fires to clear old trees and encourage new plants to grow for their food.

ENEMIES

European settlers treated the Aboriginal people badly. They said the Aboriginal lifestyle was primitive and worthless. They hunted Aboriginal people with guns, and took away their lands to create sheep farms and cattle ranches for themselves. As a result, the Aboriginal people and Europeans often fought. To try to bring peace, the British governor of Australia had this poster printed in 1816. It shows how he wanted everyone to behave toward one another. It is written in picture-language, since, at that time, many people could not read.

▲ *Aboriginal boys played with spears and boomerangs. This was good practice for hunting when they were grown up. If they lived along the coast or near a river, they also played with fishing nets and toy boats.*

▲ *On special occasions men, women, and children painted their faces and bodies in ancient, traditional designs to look like creatures from the Dreamtime. These girls are dressed and painted, ready to dance and sing the story of a magical snake.*

INDUSTRIAL ENGLAND

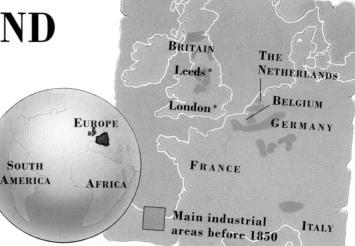

CHARLES BURNS was born in about 1818. He lived and worked in Leeds, an industrial city in northern England. When he was thirteen years old he described his life at work: "I began to work when I was eight. I worked in a flax mill. My job was to take the full bobbins [reels of thread] off the spinning machines. I worked from six in the morning till seven at night, with forty minutes' break for dinner. I had no time off for breakfast or to have a drink in the afternoon. If we stopped working, sat down, or spoke to each other, we were cruelly beaten."

"I work at another flax mill now," Charles went on. "It is very hot and dusty. The machines splash water around, so the air is full of steam and my clothes get soaked. In winter, when I walk home, my clothes freeze and stick to my skin. The work has made me ill. My throat hurts. I cough and spit up blood. There are often accidents at the mill. My sister was killed in one."

▲ The first factories were built in the Midlands and northwest England, between 1770 and 1800. During the next hundred years, factories spread to many parts of Europe. They were usually built close to sources of power and raw materials, such as water, coal, and iron.

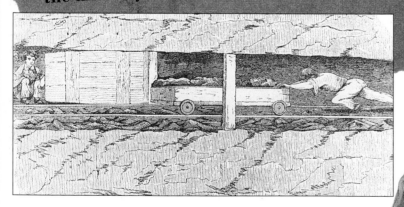

▲ Factories needed coal to provide power for their new machines. Men, women, and children worked deep underground in mines, digging coal and hauling it toward the surface by hand. Children were sent to work in the smallest spaces. The eight-year-old girl pictured above in the 1830s (on the left) spent all day crouched in a narrow tunnel. Her job was to open and close heavy trapdoors to let coal carts pass through. She sang to stop herself from feeling afraid.

FACTORIES AND MACHINES

The Industrial Revolution began in England in about 1750 when British engineers discovered how to use steam power to drive machines. Machines could produce large quantities of goods much more quickly and cheaply than people working by hand. The first machines that were built spun thread and wove it into cloth. Soon many other traditional crafts, such as brick making, ironworking, and glassblowing, were carried out by machines, too.

The new machines were housed in huge, noisy factories. Poor families left their homes in the countryside and moved to the towns that were built near the factories, in the hope of finding jobs. But factory towns were crowded and full of disease. Most workers' houses had no heating, no clean water supplies, and no drains, and workers could not afford to pay doctors' fees when they or their children became ill.

▼ *There was no free state education in England before 1870. Many poor children received hardly any education at all. To help them, charities set up free "Ragged Schools" where they could go after their day's work to learn reading, writing, and math.*

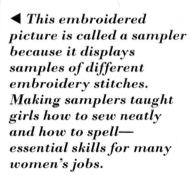

◄ *This embroidered picture is called a sampler because it displays samples of different embroidery stitches. Making samplers taught girls how to sew neatly and how to spell— essential skills for many women's jobs.*

▼ *Like the millions of other children working in factories across Europe, Charles Burns was cheap to employ since his wages were lower than an adult's. Children were also small enough to crawl inside big machines, like these looms, to clean them or sweep up beneath them. Many terrible accidents happened when children got trapped in the machines.*

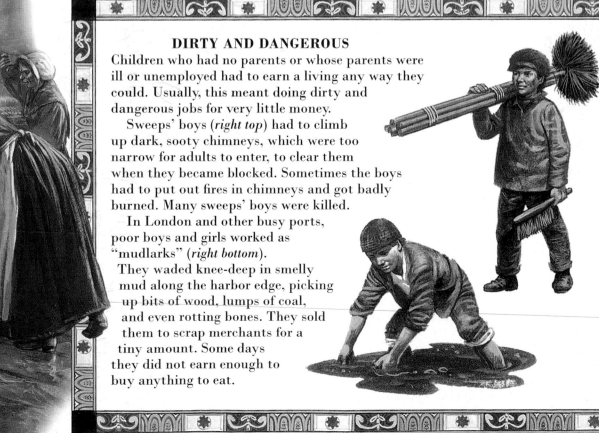

DIRTY AND DANGEROUS

Children who had no parents or whose parents were ill or unemployed had to earn a living any way they could. Usually, this meant doing dirty and dangerous jobs for very little money.

Sweeps' boys (*right top*) had to climb up dark, sooty chimneys, which were too narrow for adults to enter, to clear them when they became blocked. Sometimes the boys had to put out fires in chimneys and got badly burned. Many sweeps' boys were killed.

In London and other busy ports, poor boys and girls worked as "mudlarks" (*right bottom*). They waded knee-deep in smelly mud along the harbor edge, picking up bits of wood, lumps of coal, and even rotting bones. They sold them to scrap merchants for a tiny amount. Some days they did not earn enough to buy anything to eat.

WORLD WAR II

Anne Frank in 1942, at about age thirteen

Lands occupied by Germany 1940–1945

Lands fighting against Germany

Germany and its allies

THE NETHERLANDS

Amsterdam

GERMANY

U.S.S.R.

EUROPE

EUROPE

▲ German troops invaded and occupied much of Europe. Many other countries, such as America, Australia, and Japan, also became involved.

ANNE FRANK was four years old when Adolf Hitler (see page 51) came to power in Germany in 1933. Anne's family was Jewish, so they moved from Germany to the Netherlands, where they hoped they would be safe from Hitler's attacks on Jewish people. But German soldiers invaded the Netherlands in 1940. Anne's parents decided that the only way to keep their family safe was to hide them away. Early one morning in July 1942, Anne and her family crept out of their house in Amsterdam and went to hide in four rooms tucked away behind her father's office. They did not leave these rooms for two years. For most of the time nobody dared move or make a noise. A few friends risked their lives to bring the family food.

But in the summer of 1944, the family was discovered. German soldiers arrested them and sent them to prison camps in Germany where Anne, her mother, and sister died from hunger and disease. Anne died in March 1945 at the age of fifteen.

▶ Anne kept a diary while her family was in hiding. In it she wrote letters to an imaginary friend called Kitty, describing what was happening to her family, and her own hopes and fears.

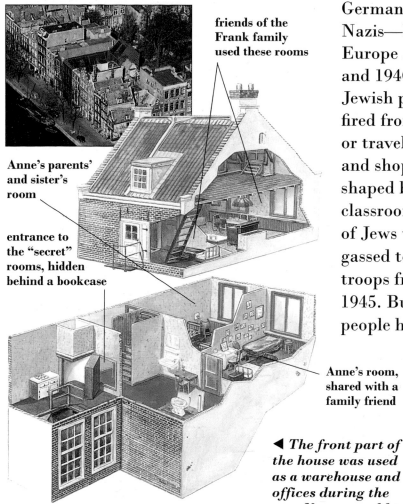

▼ *Like many old Dutch houses, the building where Anne Frank's family hid was squeezed onto a narrow site.*

friends of the Frank family used these rooms

Anne's parents' and sister's room

entrance to the "secret" rooms, hidden behind a bookcase

Anne's room, shared with a family friend

◀ *The front part of the house was used as a warehouse and offices during the war. No one could tell that there was a jumble of oddly shaped rooms, attics, and passageways at the back of the building (pictured). This made it possible for Anne and her family to hide there.*

HITLER AND THE JEWS

Adolf Hitler became head of the government of Germany in 1933. He and his supporters—called Nazis—had two main aims: to conquer more land in Europe and to get rid of all Jewish people. In 1939 and 1940, Hitler's troops invaded much of Europe. Jewish people in German-occupied countries were fired from government jobs, stopped from driving cars or traveling on buses, banned from theaters, cinemas, and shops, and were made to wear a big yellow star-shaped badge. Jewish children were taken from their classrooms and were sent to separate schools. Millions of Jews were sent to prison camps, where many were gassed to death. Germany was finally defeated by troops from Britain, France, Russia, and America in 1945. But by that time about six million Jewish people had been killed.

CHILDREN IN WAR

Children throughout Europe suffered during the war. Many Jewish children spent years in hiding before being found and killed. Some were smuggled out of German-occupied countries and sent to live with strangers in distant lands. Most of them never saw their parents again.

Many other children lost their fathers—between 1939 and 1945 about fifteen million men were killed—and children in big cities were often killed or badly injured by bombs. This young girl (*above*) was rescued from the ruins of her bombed home in London, England.

▼ *The Germans ordered Jews to report for duty at "work camps" in Germany. Whole families were rounded up and loaded onto trains. The camps were in fact terrible prisons where millions of Jews were killed. If Jews refused to go or hid away, German soldiers searched for them, raided their homes, and arrested them.*

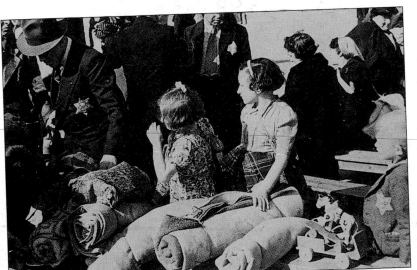

FROM CRADLE TO GRAVE

CHILDREN HAVE BEEN BROUGHT UP IN different ways across the world and through the generations. Parents try to keep their children healthy and prepare them for the adult lives they will lead.

Some ideas about raising children have changed little over the centuries. Few people today give their babies lucky charms quite like Native American turtle amulets (*see right*). But young children in many parts of the world are given a "lucky" silver coin or a necklace with a religious pendant, such as a Christian cross or a Jewish Star of David, by relatives who hope it will keep them safe.

Other ideas about childcare have changed because of advances in science and medicine. We now know that strong, straight bones are produced by eating good food, not by wrapping cloth tightly around a baby's legs (*see page 53*). In the past, parents tried many different ways—such as prayers, herbs, and magic charms—to protect their children from dangerous diseases. Often, these did not work. But the practice of immunization (*see page 53*) has saved millions of children from deadly diseases since the late eighteenth century.

▲ *To protect their babies, Native American mothers made amulets (lucky charms) shaped like turtles and lizards—both symbols of long life. This turtle amulet was made in the nineteenth century.*

▶ *There were often food shortages in Aztec lands, so parents tried to make sure that their children got enough to eat. This picture copied from an Aztec codex of about 1550 shows a mother teaching her daughter to clean. Above the girl is the number of tortillas (large pancakes made from maize) that the girl should eat every day.*

▲ *The Native American Hopi nation held special tests to mark the end of a person's childhood. This girl can wear her hair in a special style to show everyone that she has passed tests in cooking, childcare, and craft skills, and is ready for marriage.*

▼ In 1796, the English doctor Edward Jenner found a way of stopping children from catching a deadly disease called smallpox by injecting them with a small dose of a similar, but weaker, disease. This helped children build an immunity to the stronger version. This treatment became known as immunization.

▲ These women bathing their babies lived in the Chinese emperor's palace in about 1200. Only wealthy families had hot water and warm rooms. In cold countries, ordinary families often didn't bathe their babies except in the warmest weather, in case they caught a cold and became seriously ill.

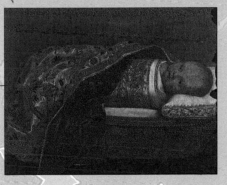

▲ In parts of Europe in the seventeenth century, mothers believed that wrapping their babies tightly in strips of linen (called "swaddling bands") would help their legs grow straight and strong.

◀ In the past, some nations believed that if a pregnant woman saw ugly things her baby would be ugly. Pregnant women from the Ashanti kingdom in west Africa gazed at little dolls, which were carved to look like beautiful people, in the hope that their babies would be beautiful, too. The dolls pictured here date from the nineteenth century.

INDEPENDENCE FOR INDIA

INDER MALHOTRA lived in the Punjab region of northwest India. In 1945 he was fifteen years old and was studying in the small town of Sangrur. Inder was very interested in politics and believed that India should no longer be ruled by Britain.

One day Inder and his fellow students heard that Jawaharlal Nehru, a leading campaigner for India's independence, had been arrested. The students were furious. As a protest they decided to stop studying and go on strike. Inder went to the college principal and said, "Sorry but today there can be no work. . . . We're going on a march to the office of the police chief to demand that Mr. Nehru be released at once."

The students rushed to the police station, shouting and waving their fists. Years later, Inder remembered, "We hoped to be arrested and were very anxious that we should at least spend a few days in jail." But the police chief was kind and explained to the students that he simply didn't have the authority to set Nehru free. Inder remembers, "We shouted a few more slogans and came back to the college. We tried once or twice to get arrested but it did not work."

▼ In 1947 British India was divided into two new nations called India and Pakistan. They were created so that the two largest religious groups, the Hindus and the Muslims, could each have a homeland where they could speak their own language and obey their own religious laws.

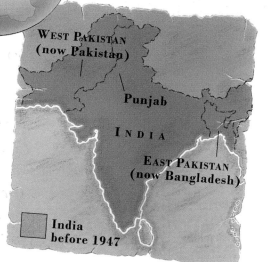

ASIA

INDIA

WEST PAKISTAN (now Pakistan)

Punjab

I N D I A

EAST PAKISTAN (now Bangladesh)

India before 1947

▲ Bombay Railway Station, built in about 1866, was a symbol of British India. It was built for steam trains, which were invented by the British, but was designed in an Indian style and staffed by skilled Indian workers.

▶ *India was home to people with many different languages and religious beliefs. Most people were Hindus, but there were also Muslims, Buddhists, Sikhs, Parsees, and Jains. Finding a way for them all to live together peacefully was a huge challenge for the new Indian government after 1947.*

▲ *Mohandas Gandhi (1869–1948) devoted his life to non-violent protests against British rule. He encouraged ordinary people to stand up for what they believed was right and to protest peacefully for India's independence.*

BRITAIN AND INDIA

Since 1858, Britain had ruled India. Many Indian people disliked British rule and wanted to be free to run their own country.

Although the British had built roads and railways across India and had given Indian people training for jobs in offices and factories, they had brought these changes mainly to help British industries. The British introduced taxes on land, which Indian farmers found difficult to pay. They also closed down many Indian cotton mills because these took business away from mills in Britain.

From 1885, politicians began to demand India's independence. These demands increased after the Amritsar Massacre of 1919, when British troops fired on unarmed protestors, killing 379 and seriously injuring nearly 1,200. Britain was finally forced to give India its independence in 1947.

◀ *Inder Malhotra and his fellow students refused to study when they heard that Jawaharlal Nehru had been arrested. They marched to the police station to protest. A number of them wanted to be put in jail in the hope that it would increase support for Nehru and for India's independence.*

POLITICAL LEADERS

India gained its independence largely through the work of Mohandas Gandhi (*see above left*) and two great political campaigners, Jawaharlal Nehru (1889–1964), and Mohammed Ali Jinnah (1876–1948). Nehru (*bottom left*) was leader of the Indian National Congress, a powerful political party. He called for independence in speeches and writings and was arrested by the British many times. He became the first prime minister of independent India in 1947. Jinnah (*bottom right*) was leader of a political party called the Muslim League, which wanted a separate state where Indian Muslims could live. Jinnah became the first prime minister of the new Muslim country of Pakistan.

THE END OF APARTHEID

Khayakazi Khatwya at the age of fifteen

KHAYAKAZI KHATWYA was eleven years old on April 27, 1994, when apartheid finally ended and black South Africans won the right to vote. This is how she describes that day. "To be honest, I did not know what to expect, but I knew it was something big. At my home, everyone was very excited, especially my parents. When they went to vote, the queues [lines] were very long. I went there, too. Everyone was talking about the vote and cars were honking like mad. I wanted to vote, but I was too young. Then my mother discovered that she did not have her identity document with her. She would have to show this before she could vote. She was so shocked. She sent me to get it. I ran so fast that I did not feel the distance. I did not want her to lose her chance to vote because I knew how important it was for her and for me. When I came back with the document my mother was so relieved and I felt so proud of what I did. It was as if I voted myself."

▲ South Africa is a vast, rich country. Until 1994, the government allowed only white people to own almost all the good land and big businesses.

▼ *After 1950, black people were not allowed to live in the cities, so many moved to crowded workers' townships like this. Most houses in the townships had no water or electricity and there were few schools or hospitals.*

▼ *Wednesday April 27, 1994, was the first time all South African citizens were free to vote to choose their government. Khayakazi Khatwya and her family joined the crowds of people waiting patiently for hours outside the polling station where they would vote.*

BLACK AND WHITE

South Africa is home to many different peoples—African, Indian, "coloreds" (people born to parents from different ethnic groups), and "whites" (the descendants of European settlers, who arrived after 1700). Africans, Indians, and colored people are often called "blacks." They make up more than eighty percent of South Africa's population.

South Africa is a rich country, with huge deposits of gold and diamonds. But its black people have lived in poverty and have been badly treated and misunderstood by its white people, who have enjoyed one of the highest living standards in the world. Now, however, President Mandela's new government has promised to give all South African people—black and white—the chance for a good education, better housing and health care, and fair shares in their country's wealth.

▲ *Nelson Mandela was leader of the ANC (African National Congress), the main political party fighting against apartheid. He was put in prison by the white government of South Africa in 1962 and spent twenty-seven years there. He became the first black president of South Africa following the elections on April 27, 1994.*

APARTHEID

The word apartheid means "apartness." It was a very unfair political system, which treated people differently because of the color of their skin. Apartheid was started in 1948 by the government of South Africa, which was controlled by whites. They believed that they were better and more clever than blacks. Under apartheid, white people had the best housing, education, jobs, and medical care. Black people did not have the right to vote. They were not allowed to use the same schools, hospitals, or trains as white people, or to sit in places that were for "whites only."

◄ *There were many protests against apartheid in South Africa. In 1976, students in Soweto, near Johannesburg, protested against the government's plans to make Afrikaans—the language spoken by most whites—the only language used in schools. Pupils wanted to be taught in English or their own African languages. Many of the students were shot and killed by soldiers and police.*

TIME LINE

1500 B.C. 1100 700 300 A.D. 1 100 200 300 400 500 600 700 800

The children discussed in this book represent a great many time periods, but they barely address the vast amount of our world's history. This time line places the children's stories—indicated here by the larger dates—alongside the important events that influenced their lives.

3100–30 B.C. Ancient Egyptian civilization is rich and powerful.

753 B.C. City of Rome is founded.

2000 B.C.–A.D. 200 Roman civilization is at its most powerful.

1489 B.C. Tuthmosis III becomes pharaoh of Egypt at the age of ten. His stepmother Queen Hatshepsut rules instead of him until 1469 B.C. Tuthmosis reigns until 1436 B.C.

c. 750–350 B.C. "Golden Age" of ancient Greek civilization.

776 B.C. First-ever Olympic Games are held in Greece.

463 B.C. Boy athlete Alcimidas wins famous victory in wrestling contest at Nemean Games in Greece. Greek poet Pindar writes a special poem to praise him.

A.D. 79 Roman teenager Pliny the Younger witnesses eruption of volcano Vesuvius on August 24. He writes about the disaster in letters, which we can still read today.

c. A.D. 400 Beginning of first Mongol Empire in Asia.

c. A.D. 105 Paper is first used in China.

A.D. 250–900 Mayan civilization in Mexico is at its richest and most powerful.

A.D. 615 Lord Pacal becomes ruler of Mayan city-state of Palenque when he is twelve years old. His reign lasts for sixty-eight years.

A.D. 476 Final collapse of Roman power.

A.D. 330 Capital of Roman empire is moved from Rome to Constantinople (now Istanbul) in Turkey.

A.D. 800–1100 The Viking Age in northern Europe. Viking sailors from Scandinavia explore and settle in many northern lands.

A.D. 870 Vikings discover Iceland.

A.D. 758 Muslim Princess Zubaidah born in Baghdad. She grows up to marry Caliph Harun al-Rashid and becomes a wise and generous queen.

A.D. 732–1258 Muslim caliphs of Baghdad rule a vast empire in Middle East.

A.D. 762 City of Baghdad founded by Caliph al-Mansūr in present-day Iraq.

1500 B.C. 1100 700 300 A.D. 1 100 200 300 400 500 600 700 800

900　1000　1100　1200　1300　1400　1500　1600　1700　1800　1900　2000

1050
Bold Viking boy Egil Skallagrimsson lives around this time. He joins Viking raids and becomes a famous poet.

c. 1440
Young prince Ogun of the west African kingdom of Benin returns from hiding to become Oba (king) of Benin.

1789
The French Revolution begins, witnessed by eleven-year-old Marie-Victoire Monnard. Thousands of people in France, including its king and queen, are executed before the Revolution ends in 1795.

1438–1532
The Incas rule an empire high in the Andes Mountains of South America. They are famous for their roads, huge stone buildings, and fine gold and silver work.

1994
Eleven-year-old Khayakazi Khatwya witnesses the end of apartheid in South Africa.

1001
Vikings land in America.

1813
Native American boy Mistippee is born into the Creek people living in the southeast of North America.

A.D. 960–1279
Song dynasty reigns in China. Chinese inventions and discoveries make China the most advanced civilization in the world.

1620
English girl Mary Allerton sails with many other Pilgrims to a new life in America.

GEORGE WASHINGTON PRESIDENT 1793

1212
French shepherd boy Stephen of Cloyes leads a children's crusade in France.

1325–1519
Aztec civilization flourishes in what is now Mexico.

1587
Birth of Nathan Field, famous English boy actor.

1832
Aboriginal girl Ballandella is born in southeast Australia.

1096–1291
The Crusades—Holy Wars between Christians and Muslims—are fought in the Middle East.

1471
Albrecht Dürer is born. He becomes the most famous German artist of Renaissance times.

1929
Jewish girl Anne Frank is born in Germany. She dies in a German prison camp in 1945 at the age of fifteen.

1939–1945
World War II. Many nations join the fight against Adolf Hitler, head of the German government and leader of the Nazi Party.

c. 1400–1550
The Renaissance era in Europe—a time of new ideas and great achievements in art, architecture, music, literature, and learning.

1818
Charles Burns is born in industrial city of Leeds in England. He starts work in a mill at the age of eight.

1947
India gains independence from British rule.

c. 1265
Mongol Princess Aiyaruk is born in East Asia. She grows up to become a famous warrior.

1750–1850
The Industrial Revolution in Europe. Many scientific discoveries are made and new machines invented.

A.D. 1206–1227
Genghis Kahn is leader of all Mongol tribes. Mongol armies conquer a vast empire in Asia, eastern Europe, and the Middle East.

1945
Inder Malhotra and his fellow students at a college in India go on strike in support of India's independence.

900　1000　1100　1200　1300　1400　1500　1600　1700　1800　1900　2000

INDEX

Note: Page numbers in *italic* refer to information given only in boxes or picture captions or labels.

T
toys *14–15, 25, 47*
Trail of Tears *45*
Tuthmosis III, Pharaoh *6, 8, 9, 58*

U V
Vikings *20–21, 58, 59*

W
work (children's) *7, 11, 21, 26, 35, 41, 42–43, 44, 48–49*

World War II *50–51, 59*
writing *6–7, 8, 9, 13, 17*
glyphs (Mayan) *17*
hieroglyphics (Egyptian) *8*

X Y Z
Zubaidah *18, 19, 58*

GLOSSARY

ancient *A period in history very long ago, usually said to be before about A.D. 476.*

city-state *A city and its surrounding lands, villages, and farms that make up a separate state within a country.*

civil war *A war between people from the same country.*

colonies *Settlements in one country of people from another country, who remain governed or ruled by their native country.*

democratic *A system of government in which all the adults in the country have a say in how it is run, usually by choosing who will represent them in the government.*

emigrate *To leave one's native country to go to live in another country.*

inscriptions *Words that are written or carved on any material such as metal, stone, or paper. Inscriptions may use letters or pictures to represent the words.*

medieval *A period in history, usually said to be between about A.D. 476 and about A.D. 1500.*

native *(especially native peoples) People who were born in the country in which they live.*

nomads *Peoples who do not live in one place but move from camp to camp, usually to find new sources of food.*

Persia *A country in southwest Asia, known as Iran since 1935. People from here were known as Persians.*

scribes *People who wrote documents and official records in the past. Scribes wrote everything by hand.*

taxes *Money that people have to give to their government or ruler.*

ACKNOWLEDGMENTS

Main illustrations by: *Richard Berridge, Christian Hook, Roger Payne, Michael Welply, and Michael White.*

Other illustrations by: *Peter Sarson, Roger Payne, and Michael White*

Photographic credits:
(t=top, b=bottom, l=left, r=right, c=center)
8 *tl* and 9 *tr* and *br* Peter Clayton; 10 A.K.G. *ct*; 11 A.K.G. *tr*, Peter Clayton *cl*; 13 Ancient Art & Architecture Collection *tl*, Photo Resources C.M.Dixon *br*; 14 Werner Forman Archive *ct*; 15 Bridgeman Art Library/Private Collection *tl*, Bridgeman Art Library/ Victoria & Albert Museum *tr*, British Museum EA15671 *cl*; 16 Werner Forman Archive *tl*, South American Pictures *cr*; 17 Michael Holford *tr*, British Museum 1977 Am38.1 *br*; 18 *bl* and 19 *br* Sonia Halliday Photographs; 21 E.T.Archive *tr*, Werner Forman Archive *cr*; 23 Bridgeman Art Library/Victoria & Albert Museum *cl*, Robert Harding Picture Library *cr*; 25 E.T.Archive *br*; 27 British Museum Roy.2A.XX11 fol. 220 *tr*; 28 E.T.Archive *ct*; 29 Bridgeman Art Library/ Private Collection *ct*, Panos Pictures *cr* and *cb*; 30 A.K.G *tl*; 31 A.K.G *tr* and *br*, St. Bride Printing Library *c*; 33 Bridgeman Art Library/British Museum *tl*, British Museum/The Royal Collection Her Majesty Queen Elizabeth 11 *tr*; 34 Hutchison Library/H.R.Dorig *tr*, Werner Forman Archive *br*; 37 E.T.Archive *tl*, Bridgeman Art Library/Private Collection *cr*; 39 E.T.Archive *tr*; 40 Bridgeman Art Library/Château de Versailles *bl*; 41 A.K.G *tr*; 42 Bridgeman Art Library/ British Library *cb*; 43 Faculty of Archaeology & Anthropology, Cambridge *tr*, Michael Holford *bl*, British Museum B226 *cb*; 46 The Image Library, State Library of NSW *tl*, Werner Forman Archive *br*; 47 The Image Library, State Library of NSW *bl*, Stanley Breeden *br*; 48 A.K.G *cl*; 49 Bridgeman Art Library/ Dreweatt Neate Fine Art Auctioneers, Newbury *c*; 50 AFF/AFS Amsterdam *tl*; 51 KLM Aerocarto *tl*, Rijksinstituut voor Oorlogsdocumentatie, Amsterdam *bl*, Hulton Getty Picture Collection *cr*; 52 Werner Forman Archive *tr*; 53 Freer Gallery of Art, Smithsonian Institute, Washington DC *tr*, Bridgeman Art Library/Palazzo Pitti, Florence *c*; 54 Hutchison Library *bl*; 55 Camera Press *tl*, Hulton Getty Picture Collection *br*; 56 Thembile Pepeteka *tl*, Panos Pictures *tr*; 57 Camera Press *bl* and *cr*, Cannon Collins Educational Trust for South Africa *b*.

Whenever possible, the illustrations in this book are based on surviving evidence from each child's own time. We have tried to make them as accurate as possible, but sometimes the evidence needed for every detail of our illustrations has not survived. In those cases, we have had to rely on descriptions left by people in the past and the opinions of present-day historians.